PROLOGUE

Little lamb, come to me.
The night is deep.
The storm is long.
You'll cry and scream,
but you belong to me.

HIS WINTER BABY

KATRINA YANG

CONTENTS

ONE

The folks at the last convenience store warned me not to go any farther. With the storm coming, there was simply no point in going on.

Spring in these parts doesn't come 'til April. For the snow to truly be gone? That'd be June.

You'd better go back to where you came from, sweetheart. This weather ain't for city girls who dress like you.

I rolled my eyes and told them I'd take my chances. The sky looked fine. Everyone was on their way to their families for the holidays. Even if something did happen, I figured I'd be able to find help.

I had my chains and a full tank, but in retrospect, maybe I should've listened.

The storm hit when it hit. One second, it was sunny and clear; the next, I'd turned into the mountains and found myself inside a blizzard. Even with chains, the wheels spun. The heater started blowing cold air.

I tried to pretend it was no big deal for the first couple of minutes, but the altitude kept climbing, and soon, I couldn't even see the road.

I didn't want to admit that maybe the clerk had been right, but pressing on started to feel like a really bad idea.

The dashboard lights flickered.

"Okay, this is it," I said to myself, taking a deep breath.

I pulled the gear into reverse and backed a little to the side, then shifted to drive and spun the wheel all the way to the left.

I was in the middle of the turn when the car got stuck.

I kicked the gas—and kicked it again.

It wouldn't budge.

I got out to check. Tried digging the snow with my bare hands. Got back in, kicked the gas again. Pulled the gear into reverse and tried once more.

I screamed. Hit the horn with both arms.

Nothing worked.

No matter what I did, the car stayed exactly where it was.

Well, someone else had to be coming up this way eventually. It was the holiday season. I couldn't be the only one taking this road. I mean, was there another way around? I didn't think so.

I kept the engine running, sitting in my car.

The engine died around 4 p.m.

The sky was already dark.

The snow had frozen everything solid.

I got out, took one step, and my entire lower leg sank under.

The flakes felt like blades in the harsh wind.

I trembled, putting one foot in front of the other, fighting my way back, hoping some idiot like me with a big truck would turn up.

I couldn't even feel my face.

My boots were soaked within minutes.

All I felt was irritating pain and deep shivers in my bones—cold penetrating my coats and burning deep into my skin.

I remembered snow differently, at my grandma's in Oregon. There, winter was magical—snowmen and skating, riding in my grandparents' car, looking out at a world covered in white.

Literally. Not. This.

I didn't believe I'd see a light. By the time it came, I had fallen for the fifth time, thinking I was going to die in these mountains.

It wasn't bright at first—just a blurry blob that looked unreal. But then it got clearer, brighter, and I heard the sound of an engine, chained wheels crashing through the snow, headed toward me.

I started to feel hope again.

"Help..." I lifted my head and shouted in a weak voice. My lips had stopped trembling by then. "Help..."

The truck stopped a little way off.

The door opened.

A man ran toward me.

He was around my father's age, with a mustache and thick brows, looking kind of like Sheriff Swan from *Twilight*. His eyes never once lingered on my face. Like a silent hero.

He had a warm hat and a really thick coat, properly dressed for weather like this.

He picked me up, carried me to his truck, placed me gently on the seat, wrapped me in blankets, and pressed a hat on my head.

Then he tossed me a warm rubber pouch full of hot water and shut the door.

"You're gonna be just fine," he said, climbing into the driver's seat and closing the door. He turned the heater all the way to the warmest while I shivered, clutching the warm rubber pouch.

He kicked on the gas and charged forward.

"No... don't..." I managed to squeeze a word out. "G-go... b-b-back..."

He gave me a look and hit the brakes, and words disappeared from my lips.

"The storm is only gonna get worse," he said in a low voice. "You just sit back and focus on getting warm."

I'd usually be offended by those words, but the way

he spoke reminded me of my father, who never learned how to express his feelings in a way other people could easily understand.

So when he hit the gas again, I sank back into the seat and clutched the pouch, feeling the warmth seep through my skin.

All I needed was to know I could trust him.

I did know.

He saved me, wrapped me in warm clothes, and now, he was taking me to safety. Who was I to question him?

Instead of getting in his way, I focused on stopping my teeth from making more embarrassing noises.

I flexed and opened my fingers, slowly regaining some mobility, and once he saw I did, he passed me a silver insulated bottle.

"Drink it," he said. "It'll help."

"What's in it?"

"Hot water."

I tried to twist the lid off, but it was tight.

"Every year, an idiot drives up this road, thinking they're not gonna die," he said coldly. "I had a room at the Red Motel. Thought I'd stay in town this year. Wasn't gonna make the trip, but they dragged me out, told me to drive up to my cabin because there's a girl up here who's gonna freeze to death on her way to Oregon."

"R-really?" My lips trembled.

The stranger didn't say another word. He just took

the thermos from my hand, placed it between his legs, twisted the cap off for me, poured some water into it, and handed it back.

I managed to take a sip between the quivering and the chattering, and as it rolled down my chest into my stomach, I felt, for the first time, that I had a grip on my own shivering.

"Thank you," I said.

He nodded in reply.

I didn't know if it was the rubber pouch filled with hot water on my stomach or something else, but I felt a warm stream in my heart. He came all the way up here in the worsening storm to save me. He even gave up his motel room.

The road had long disappeared. I had no idea where we were going—just that we were deeper in the mountains. The blizzard was getting worse. There was no turning back now.

It made me nervous and scared looking outside the window, so I gazed at him instead.

"What's your name?" I asked.

"My friends call me Ned."

As if trying to make me feel better, he reached into his pocket and handed me his driver's license.

Edgar Finnegan.

I looked up at him. My fingers brushed against the photo of him, taken five years ago. I didn't mean to spy, but still, I did the math in my head.

Fifty-three.

He was more than twice my age—two years older than my father.

A young girl like me probably wouldn't spark his interest.

The thought came out of nowhere.

I shook my head, a little embarrassed, telling myself to stop. But I couldn't help replaying the image of him carrying me to his truck in the snow.

He was strong, steady, and fearless—not like men my age, with their ambition and ignorance. His temperance came from years of surviving the harsh weather. He knew, not guessed or risked.

And I didn't know any man like that in my life, except my father.

"Is your wife at the motel?" I blurted out before I could stop myself.

I immediately regretted it.

He doesn't even know my name yet, and I was already asking about his marital status... Suggesting what, exactly? Why the hell did I ask?

"Shit... S-Sorry..." I stuttered, flustered. "I'm Casey, by the way. Casey Jones. And you definitely don't have to answer that."

For a second or two, he didn't say a thing, as if it was only appropriate for me to sit in my own dread.

And slowly, he talked again.

"Like the country song?" he asked. His voice was low and almost inaudible.

"Hm?"

"The country song," he said again.

He turned to look at me, as if checking whether I had heard him right, but when he caught the blankness on my face, he raised his brows.

"Never mind," he sighed.

He focused on the road again.

It almost seemed like he had something else to say, but he just decided to keep the thoughts to himself.

I handed back his ID, feeling a little left out.

And for a while, we sat in awkward silence.

"You know, your dad named you after a train driver," he said with a short chuckle, muttering mostly to himself.

"Where are you traveling from?"

This, I heard.

"San Diego."

He made a low hum in his throat, as if that explained something.

"You headed to Oregon for the holiday?" he asked. "You got any family there?"

"Yeah. My grandparents live there."

He made a face, but I didn't know what that meant.

"Let me guess—you take the plane every year, but this year you thought, *hey, why not do something stupid for a change?*" He laughed, as if my suffering was entertainment.

My face burned.

I wanted to snap something back, but the words

were caught somewhere between my throat and this stupid warmth in my chest. All I could think about was how he sounded like my father when he teased me. And I started to let go of the rubber pouch I had been squeezing so hard.

Civilization was miles behind us. We were in no man's land while the wind started to rock the truck.

I had never been this far away from home, but I felt...safe in the blankets, next to him.

My gaze landed on his face again, thinking how he was like a mountain, unmoved by the turbulence in the outside world.

My heart slowed, and all the drumming in madness and panic started to fade.

"You gotta quit looking at me like that, girl," he said softly after a while.

"Like what?" I played coy.

"Like you've got a thing for me." He made a grunting noise and shifted in the driver's seat. He reached and rubbed the back of his neck.

"Is this how men of your generation flirt?" I snapped back.

At that, he took a sharp breath in.

"How old are you?" he asked, his voice sounding a little guilty.

"Twenty-two," I whispered, not even blinking.

He made another noise, shifting in his seat again.

"I'm scared to look outside the window," I said innocently.

"Then close your eyes," he said, clearing his throat.

But I refused.

I was smiling and flushing, and I couldn't just look away.

He raised his hand and put it up between us to block my gaze.

I snuggled down in my seat, a little daring.

He kept his hand between us, the other on the wheel. I sniffed his scent on the blanket he wrapped me in, and the two of us stayed in silence as something brewed between us.

At some point, I gazed down. Between his legs, the fabric folded into a wrinkle that kind of looked like a bulge.

It was pointed in my direction, hard and a little round on the edges. It looked like something was straining the fabric underneath all the layers—and I started to bite my lip.

For a moment, I couldn't move my eyes away.

TWO

"Stay here."

He pulled the truck in front of a cabin, half-buried in the snow. He parked the truck but left the engine running so that the heater would still be on.

My eyes followed him as he opened the door and stood, trying to see whether the wrinkle had turned into a tent. He fixed his belt and walked over to pick up a shovel.

In the distance, he started to dig the front door out of the snow.

I was... rather fixated on the moment he stood up. It was too brief for me to see anything substantial, but if he was wearing tighty-whities, his reaction might not be so obvious.

I was all in my head while he worked on the front door.

After a while, he tossed the shovel aside and

unlocked the heavy wooden door. He gave it a hard push, putting his weight on it.

It wouldn't open, so he tried again.

And it worked.

He looked inside, dusting his hands, then he walked back to me.

And my heart started to race again.

"You strong enough to walk?" he asked, opening my side of the door.

I nodded.

"Okey-Dokey."

He stepped on the step, leaning over me to turn off the engine.

Then he shook the chain in his hands, looking at me.

Our eyes met, and my breath halted.

"Got the keys..." he whispered.

"Right..."

For a while, no one said a word.

"Nah. I don't think so." A frown emerged on his face. He broke eye contact, and before I could process what was going on, I felt his arms gripping my shoulders and the sides of my legs. He picked me up, kicked the door shut with his boots, and carried me toward his cabin.

"I thought I could walk by myself," I whispered.

I had my hands pressed on his chest. My eyes looked up at his jawline.

I didn't know if he heard me.

He acted like he didn't, and my heart started to feel both fast and weak.

I just knew that he dropped me gently on the floor after we went in. The door closed behind us, and for a second, before the light turned on, it was completely dark.

Only the sounds of our breathing, a little shallow and ragged. My arms were still around his neck. My fingers were tugging him closer.

His hand twisted the lock.

I swallowed, feeling both a little scared and massively turned on.

There were only the two of us.

Not another soul for miles.

A second later, he flipped the switch on.

He stood right in front of me, his eyes dark and glistening.

"Excuse me." He pressed my arms to lower them and lifted his leg, putting one foot in front of the other, and walked past me.

He stopped at the table.

"This cabin is ten miles from the main road. Once the storm hit, I ain't going into town 'til spring."

"Spring doesn't come until April," I said, biting my lip.

"That's right," he said without turning around.

I saw him reach into his pocket and take out a lighter. He clicked the lid off and held it near a long candle.

"You understand you ain't going nowhere in the next five months," he said, his voice low and a little dark, much like the cabin. "You'll die if you try."

"I know." I clutched the blankets a little tighter around me.

His thumb brushed the lighter switch, and a flame licked the candle's wick. He watched it flicker, then put the lighter on the table.

He turned to look at me briefly before heading out to the back.

I followed him and watched him split some wood.

Without another word—only the sound of our breathing, the snow falling, the twigs crackling.

He carried a bundle inside, placed it in the fireplace, then poured some gas on the kindling underneath and lit everything up.

In the sound of wood cracking, the fire started.

I moved closer to it and raised my hands to warm them.

He went off to fetch another bundle, took it into another room, and did the same.

I heard his footsteps moving between rooms.

In a little while, he carried blankets, sheets, and pillows to me.

"You're gonna sleep in there," he said, gesturing for me to come to him.

I stood up and walked into the small bedroom.

Standing behind him, my fingers slid out of the

blankets he had wrapped around me a few hours earlier.

He stretched the sheet and made the bed, then he put his knee on the mattress to tug the sheets under the mattress, smoothing them out. From the little drawer by the nightstand he took out a pair of handcuffs.

He turned, holding them in his hand.

"Get on the bed," he said, looking at me with eyes as deep as the night.

I didn't know what I was thinking.

I wasn't thinking.

I just knew that my heart skipped a beat and then started to race. I did what he told me: I put one leg on the bed, then the other. Then I sat at the edge, on my heels, looking up at him. My heart drumming, my fingers tangled together.

He gestured for me to move to the head of the bed.

So I did.

I crawled on all fours to the head of the bed, then sat up on my legs, looking up at him again.

"Hold your wrists out," he said.

I lifted both my hands, holding them out to him.

He cuffed one wrist and dragged the cuff over the bar on the headboard, then fastened the cuff around my other wrist.

"This is for your own good," he said softly. "There's not enough food. There never will be, but we'll live."

I stared at him, not believing a word he said, but

the light was too dim. I couldn't see his face clearly, let alone what he was thinking.

All I heard were his words.

"I'm used to winters like this. I don't mind the hunger, but at some point, sooner than you realize, you're gonna sneak into my kitchen like a mouse, rummaging through our supplies—and in that case, we definitely won't last for five months, which would be the good case. In the worst cases, the roads will be blocked until May."

"If you want to cuff me to the bed, cuff me. You don't have to make up excuses," I muttered, a little breathless.

He paused for a moment, looking at me as if I had just said something deeply wrong.

"You think this is a joke?"

I didn't answer. I just looked at him, with my misty eyes and clenched knees.

"Do you hunt?" I asked.

"I do." He checked the cuffs on me, then his gaze landed on me again, and this time his voice softened, as if realizing he may have been a little harsh.

"I had a room at the motel. I've got no food up here because I wasn't going to spend the winter here."

"Then an idiot tried to get herself killed, and now you're trapped in a cabin with her."

He lifted his hand and rubbed the hat from my head, but his hand slowed on its way down. His thumb landed on my cheek, and I felt it brush my skin.

"I'm scared, Ned," I muttered, moving into his touch, a little breathless.

"Don't be," he whispered. "As long as I get a bite, you'll get one too—a big one."

I bit my lower lip softly and nodded.

I caught him looking at my lower lip when I did, and my heart raced.

I knew I probably should be more alarmed by the fact that he just cuffed me to a bed, but for reasons I didn't understand, I felt something really messed up between my legs.

Especially after what he said.

THREE

He stood by the bed and looked at me for a little longer, and then he turned and walked out.

I heard him fixing something in the kitchen. He went outside a few times, and I heard him digging in the snow with his shovel.

It didn't take long before the smell of food started to make my stomach wail, and with the fire in my room, I felt a little warm.

I couldn't take off my burgundy coat without him uncuffing me, so I kicked my boots off, and in a little while, he entered my room holding two bowls in his hands. He placed them on the nightstand and went out.

When he returned, he had forks and spoons in his hands.

He took a little chair and placed it right next to me.

He picked up the bowl and stirred the soup with a

spoon, then scooped a bit of meat and sent it to his lips, but he didn't eat it. He blew on it for a little while and held it to me.

"What is it?" I asked.

"Deer," he said. "I caught it in the summer."

I parted my lips. He sent the spoon in. I closed my mouth, and he pulled the spoon out from between my lips.

It was a little salty, but delicious.

"It's good," I said.

He raised his brow in approval and got me a bigger piece this time. He blew on it as well and sent it between my lips.

"You ever had deer before?"

"No." I shook my head. "I don't really know any hunters."

He made a noise through his nose and fed me some more, and that summed up all the meat in the bowl. The rest was just vegetables and the soup. I looked at his bowl, and unlike mine, there were only two small pieces.

Like he said, he gave me the bigger bowl.

I had already been sweating in my layers, but I didn't say a word when he fed me. Now that I had some food in my stomach, I was getting increasingly hot.

"Can I take off my coat?" I asked gently.

He hesitated, but nodded anyway. He put down his bowl of soup and unlocked the cuffs for me.

As he watched, I took my coat off, and then my sweater, and then the hoodie, until I was in a thin V-neck long-sleeve shirt.

I waved my arms to dry my sweat.

I caught him watching me, and a wild idea came to my mind.

I bit my lip slightly, reached back, and unhooked my bra from underneath the shirt. I slipped the straps from my sleeves and removed it. And there I was, braless, in front of him.

I wrapped my arms around myself to hide the fact that my nipples were poking through the fabric, but while I did, I made my breasts look even fuller.

He was... staring at the right places.

I held my wrists out to him again, but he didn't even seem to notice.

Instead, he reached for the bowl of soup and placed it in my hands.

"Eat," he said, staring at my chest. "You're too skinny."

"Says the guy who's scared of me stealing his food," I said with a chuckle.

I held up the bowl and chugged the rest.

When I finished, I caught him swallowing at the shape of my nipples.

"Still hungry?" he asked.

I nodded.

"I'll get you some more."

"I thought you didn't have more."

He didn't reply.

He stood up quickly. The chair almost fell. He tried to catch it, then immediately realized something and pressed on his crotch. This time, I didn't have to wonder. I saw it—big and hard, stretching the fabric, clearly for me.

He tugged his erection under his belt and walked out with my bowl. When he came back, there was more soup in mine and one small piece of venison.

He handed me the bowl but didn't sit down. He just watched me eat while standing in front of me. Then he took the bowl from me and put the cuffs on my wrists.

He took both bowls out, and in a little bit, he came back holding a violet dress, a toothbrush, and tooth-paste. He placed everything next to me and crouched down to unlock me.

"I thought you might want to wear something more comfortable," he said, putting the dress in my hands. "It belongs to one of my daughters. She left it here after last winter."

"How old is she?" I asked.

"Older than you," he said.

He placed the toothbrush and toothpaste in my hands and sat down in the chair. I went into the bath-room to clean myself before bed. I thought about locking the door, but I left a little crack open.

I took off everything and put on the dress.

Then, I looked at myself in the mirror.

My eyes drifted toward the door.

Our eyes met briefly before both of us looked away.

Violet was a good color on me, though the dress would look better if I could curl my hair. I played with the edge of my hair a little and decided to tie it in a braid.

I knew he'd watched the whole process, but even then, he seemed a little stunned when I came out. For a moment, he couldn't move his eyes away from me. His Adam's apple dipped and lifted.

I walked back to the bed and sat down in front of him, holding up my wrists.

He cuffed me to the bed, breathing loudly, and when it was done, he stood up. A tent strained against his pants in the most daring way possible, but he didn't move an inch, nor did he try to hide it. I looked up at him.

This time, I saw something raw and intense in his eyes—like he wanted me in ways he shouldn't.

He brushed a strand of hair behind my ear, but his hand lingered when it returned to my chin.

He tipped it gently, making me look at him.

I bit my lower lip, and his eyes tensed. He reached to free it from my teeth, his thumb brushing slowly over the softness.

I felt him tracing the shape of my mouth and the fullness of it.

I moaned when he pressed on my upper lip to loosen my jaw. My knees drew together.

A low sound rumbled in his throat as he slipped his thumb past my lips, then he pulled it back, dragging moisture across the seam. He went in again, deeper this time, and pressed down on my tongue, a little possessively. I closed my mouth, sucking him while my legs shut tight together.

My fingers clutched the dress.

His eyes tensed as he started to thrust in and out of my lips faster and rougher.

I heard him take a sharp breath.

He pulled his thumb back and picked up the bowl and my clothes, heading to the door.

"Wait…" I stopped him, feeling a little undone.

He paused, his breath ragged and fast.

"No." He slammed the door behind him.

I let out a moan in frustration, falling back onto the bed.

My heart was still racing, and I could still taste his thumb on my tongue. I pressed my face to the sheets and squeezed my legs together, aching for some kind of release, but the slick heat between my thighs only worsened.

Then I realized both my hands were cuffed to the head of the bed, and there was no way I could touch myself at night…

"Eh…" I wailed in frustration.

I knew what I was thinking was wrong on so many levels. I should've been glad he didn't fuck me the night he brought me here. Imagine what these five months would be like if he turned out to be some twisted mountain man who kept girls in chains during the winter to bear his children.

And yet... the very thought of him doing exactly that to me sent another tingling shiver between my legs.

I must have gone crazy...

All night, I twisted and turned, haunted by the way he'd touched my lips while the storm thickened outside.

Inside, it was warm and a little sweaty.

For some reason, the fact that he'd taken all my belongings didn't hit me until much later.

FOUR

I HAD FALLEN ASLEEP AT SOME POINT.

There was a strange noise at the door. Quiet and discreet. Like a soft bend of wood and a gentle twist on the knob. I told myself it was probably just the sound of old houses or Ned using the facility and kept my eyes closed.

I was almost asleep again when more noises were heard.

Louder this time.

They sounded like footsteps.

In my room.

Moving in my direction.

"Ned?" I whispered, my voice soft and wet.

I blinked hard and opened my eyes wide.

In the dark, I saw a man about Ned's height. Antlers stuck out from his head. It was a figure, a shadow, lurking in the corner. Something monstrous. Something that was...not exactly men.

Whoever — or whatever — it was didn't respond to my calling. He kept moving toward me, to the side of the bed.

Then I felt the mattress sink.

He dropped his knee onto the bed and leaned forward. His hands reached far. And I watched him crawl, slowly and monstrously, from the foot of the bed to me.

He hovered over me.

His fingers tugged my dress, folding it up my thighs, his touch cold and leathery, like gloves.

My heart raced.

My legs curled.

I felt him caressing my skin, his palms drawing slow circles around my knees before parting them wide.

He placed my legs on each side of his body. His hand brushed against my skin, moving down my thighs, rolling up the edge of the dress to reveal more skin.

Suddenly, his grip tightened. He pulled me down the bed toward him sharply. My upper thighs hit his crotch, and there was immediate pressure against my tenderest place.

Breathy noises of lust spilled out of my quivering lips.

My blood boiled.

My breath thickened.

My hands were still cuffed to the bed, my arms pulled up over my head. I was soft and defenseless, terrified, but how strongly I felt — an intense sensation rose in my lower body.

He leaned down, the mask pressing against my forehead. His hand roughed up the side of my leg under my dress, clamping my hips to his hardness. His other hand grasped my breast, claiming it as his.

My wrists strained at the cuffs. A gasp slipped from my parted lips.

He ravaged me, growling, squeezing, and grinding. His knuckles circled my nipple and pinched it real hard. At that, moans came louder from my lips.

I arched my neck, feeling a violent pulse radiating down my belly to the hard shape thrusting against my soaked panties. He reached down and unzipped his pants, and slapped that hard shape against my bare skin, hot and wet.

But it wasn't his skin I felt. Latex, again.

A small frustration bubbled in my chest.

He pressed his cock down against my entrance, his fingers twisting my panties. As I gazed at him with parted lips, he held my waist and slammed me to him. A forced stretch squeezed a scream out of me. My panties strained, and pain caught.

I was barely able to grasp what was happening when he tore the neck of the dress open. I gasped. His gloved hand climbed to hold my neck, muting the sound.

And with a muffled cry caught in my chest, he mounted me like an animal. Every thrust was deep and sudden, accompanied by a low growl. Fear dissipated faster than I could process.

Every thrust felt like an erotic shock to my nerves, spreading to my entire body. My toes curled. Tears formed at the edge of my eyes. I was half-fainting and arching, my legs spasming, my skin covered in soft sweat. And all I could do was pull the cuffs, groaning in heat as he took me to some place I had never been in my life.

He kept the pace. Not a drop faster. Not a drop slower. Just hard, wet thuds that hit deep and loud.

I shook like a leaf, digging into my own palms. Weak, exhausted, and undone.

The bed wailed.

The floor cracked.

I looked deep into the eyes behind the mask, my gaze tender and tearful.

He pulled out of me all of a sudden and flipped me to lie on my stomach.

Then I felt a hand pressing my face to the pillow.

The sound of plastic breaking could be heard from behind, followed by something light and slick hitting the ground.

My lips were lifted again, jerked to him, and he entered me, harder and deeper. At that, a low moan was caught in both of our chests.

My pussy gripped his cock tightly, skin to skin at

last, and there was a closeness between us that felt intoxicating. He drew a sharp breath in, and for a moment, we were locked together, unable to separate.

It wasn't until I felt pressure on my head that he started mounting me again in a punishing manner

"You... you have to... pull out..." I begged.

The sound of him fucking me echoed between the walls. I started to feel really faint as this deep pulse kept building at the point of impact.

"Don't come inside me... No..."

The thought of him coming so deep in me made my womb quiver.

"Please pull out..." I whimpered.

"I can't be pregnant yet. Please..."

I was in tears. So close. So raw.

His silent denial was only fuel to my fire.

A few hard thrusts later, I collapsed tearfully underneath him, heavy and hard. My body bent and softened. My core forever branded by the imaginary ejaculation. He lifted me up and slammed into me harder a few more times, and I felt his movements ease.

Thick slickness dripped down both my legs.

He gave me one last loving hump before pulling out. He zipped up his pants, and out he went.

The door was slammed shut behind him.

I lay in the semi-wet bed in a torn dress, out of breath, shocked, and completely ruined.

Even though I could smell his scent on my skin and

feel his creamy white cum leaking between my legs, I wasn't sure if it really happened or not.

It felt surreal.

Too intense to be true.

Did he really come into my room and fuck me brainless in a deer mask?

Did that really happen?

He was wearing a condom in his pants.

How odd...

And yet, I had proof.

So perhaps it was me who couldn't wrap my head around this.

FIVE

That night, he woke me up again and again.
He turned me onto my stomach, mounted me from the
back, until there was nothing but slick ruin between us.

All three times, he didn't say a single word.

No soft touches. No caresses. No cuddles. Just the
sound of our flesh colliding in delirium.

The third time he came into my room, I moaned at
the sight of his antlers, my hips pushed toward him
before his pants were even down.

And the collision felt more like a reunion — all the
yearning and pain crashing into one place.

I came twice, still begging him the same, with tears
in my voice — though those words that spilled from my
lips turned me on like a shortcut to my burning loins.

The way he fucked me wasn't sex.

It was a breeding ritual.

He was branding me.

Claiming me.

In a messed-up way, I loved every bit of it.

My bum burned so much in the morning I couldn't lie on my back, and my pussy felt raw and pulsing — and yet, every time I thought of the antlers, that wild pull surged again in my belly.

I kept tightening my legs, thinking about the triple cream pie he'd left on me — and how he'd reached down with his fingers and rubbed his cum on my lips, making me taste him.

And I... I licked my lips and took his fingers in my mouth like a needy little slut.

I couldn't quite put two and two together — the man who rescued me during the day and the antler-masked man who fucked me at night.

Was it the same person? Or had I stumbled onto something truly monstrous and forbidden?

But I wasn't brave enough to jump into the rabbit hole...

The next time he came back was at night. It was stormy and dark outside again, and the logs in my fireplace had almost completely burned down.

I had been drifting in and out of sleep all day, horny and sweaty, then cold and shivery. Like I was inside a fever. A nightmare.

I couldn't shake his image out of my mind, even though my body was worn out and hurting. I kept dreaming about him. About us.

I wondered what he'd sound like when he

finally opened his mouth and what would happen when we saw each other in the daylight. Then I wonder if I had imagined him — an oddly charming gentleman, saving me in the snow, where in reality, it'd be me who found this cabin on my own.

The door opened quietly. The wooden floor cracked under his steps. He tried to be as quiet as he could while he put the wood on the ground. But still, the noises didn't escape my ears.

I propped myself up.

The blanket fell from my shoulders, revealing my breasts under the torn dress.

"Hey," I whispered.

He paused, his hand hovering over the logs.

He turned around to look at me.

His gaze fell to my chest.

The sides of my arms brushed the sides of my breasts. He stared at it as if obsessed, and I started to feel a little shy, like perhaps I should cover myself up, but a wild feeling took over because perhaps I did like him staring at me.

His Adam's apple dipped and rose.

He rubbed his hands on the side of his jeans and walked to the closet. Swinging both doors open, he stood before a closet of dresses in various styles and sizes, as if they'd once belonged to different women.

His fingers brushed by them all and stopped at a white dress. He reached for it and took it off the hanger, then he folded it in the middle and placed it gently by my pillow.

I noticed that he had tidied up his beard and mustache. His plaid shirt was tucked into his jeans. Even his hair looked more groomed than yesterday. My heart fluttered, thinking that perhaps he did all that because of me.

"Was it you last night?" I asked, tugging his sleeve, my breath a little thin, my mouth a little dry.

His hand lingered just a beat longer. His eyes darkened.

Silence seeped between us like a serpent.

For a while, no one spoke, only the sound of wood cracking and my racing heartbeat.

He walked back to the fireplace and bent to collect the logs.

A fire started.

The silence remained.

I bit my lips, not sure what to do next.

I had so many questions, and yet, I felt nervous about asking them.

He grabbed a chair and came to sit at my bedside. He took off the cuffs on my wrists, and his eyes fell on my chest again.

"Go change," he said.

There was something in his voice that told me I shouldn't disobey.

I sat up and got out of bed, taking the white dress. I went into the bathroom, closing the door.

It was when my fingers glided up to search for the lock that I realized there was never one on this door.

It slid open after I closed it.

I looked back. He had turned his chair to face me. His eyes locked on my blossom, looking a little intense.

I swallowed hard.

My heart felt loud and fast in my chest.

I didn't know what had gotten into me, but I pulled my arms out of the broken straps, sliding the dress to my ankles. And under his gaze, I stepped out of it, naked, and his.

My fingers tangled together.

I shifted my eyes to find the shower, but there wasn't one. Instead, I grabbed the toothbrush near the sink, wet it, and squeezed some toothpaste on it, then I put it in my mouth.

A squeaking noise could be heard from the chair. His footsteps drew close and eventually stopped behind me.

I looked up and saw his reflection in the mirror, slightly blurry.

I pressed my knees together, my fingers clutching the edge of the sink.

I felt him brushing the sides of my arms, slow and lingering. Then a sudden force bent me over the sink — followed by the sound of him unzipping his pants.

Heat spread from between my legs, shameful and secret. Chloride burned in my mouth.

I must be crazy to think this was hot.

"No..." A trembling sound came out of my mouth.

"No?" he echoed, sounding a little shocked and really dangerous.

I bit my lip, but a soft moan escaped anyway.

"You wanted to talk about what happened last night." He pulled out his cock and slapped it against my slick pussy. "Now, let's talk."

A whimper trembled from my parted lips.

He grabbed my hand and pressed it to his cock, thick, veiny, and pulsing. He moved my palm up and down the shaft, then around the tip, already dripping for me.

"You want it in your cunt, don't you?" he said, giving my breast a hard squeeze. "Don't think I didn't feel how hard you came last night."

"No..." I gasped, trying to pull my hand away, but he tightened his grip and fucked it harder.

His breathing grew heavier. Louder.

Then he let go, yanked me closer, and shoved his fingers inside me, rough, fast, and aching.

And I... purred like a kitten. My face flushed.

"Next time you want to say no to me, you should say it more convincingly," he warned.

He pulled his fingers out, and I felt the head of his hot, thick cock pressed to my pussy, edging in.

He yanked my hair, and his voice growled in my ear.

"I had my way with you three times last night. I'll have my way with you today, tomorrow, and every single day for the rest of this winter. You're mine. You get that?"

I nodded. My lips trembled with fear and desire. I didn't even realize I was moving my hips, trying to swallow him deeper as my body remembered every trembling collision from the night before.

He kept just the tip in, holding it there a little longer, letting my lustful noises and soft gasps hang in the air. My pussy clenched around him, aching for release.

And then... he let go of me.

A scream tore from my throat as he thrust into me. He gripped me by the shoulder and pressed my face to the mirror. My hands braced against the edge of the sink, meeting his thrusts with a feverish mix of desire and self-destruction.

"You can scream as loud as you want. No one can hear you in these parts." His voice was hot and dangerous. His breath splashed across my neck like a drug.

Wetness dripped from between my thighs, pooling on the floor.

"Did you plan this?" I managed to gasp. My pussy clutched hard at the question, as if craving the answer.

His hand rose to my neck.

He spat the words with a sneer of pity:

"What do you think, sweetheart?"

"I think..." A moan slipped through my lips.

His thrusts deepened, driving the answer straight into me.

"I think... You abducted me..."

He wove his fingers into my hair, gripping tight. He took a deep inhale and pressed his face against mine. Then he mounted me, even harder.

"You think right."

My legs shook. Trembling moans spilled out like cries.

A few seconds later, a low groan stuttered and broke — and he emptied inside me.

He zipped up his pants and picked up my toothbrush from the sink, setting it back like nothing had happened.

Then he dragged me by my wrists to the head of the bed and cuffed me there again.

"We'd better not talk about what happens in the dark," he said, his voice lush and low.

He patted on the wall, and then he was out.

SIX

HE CARRIED A POT OF HOT WATER AND A WHITE
towel the next day.

He grabbed a chair and sat down at my bedside,
then picked up the towel and soaked it in the water. He
caught my foot, forcing my curled legs to straighten.
When I tried to pull it back, a sharp spank landed on
my leg...

At that, I stopped wiggling.

He held my foot in one hand and pressed the hot,
wet towel to the back of it. He wiped with great care
and folded the towel around my toes.

He held my foot in his hands for two long breaths,
and I started to feel a little shy and nervous because no
one had ever touched me there before. Not even my
parents. And when the towel moved down to the
bottom of my foot, my breath quickened.

He brushed it around my ankle, holding my big

toe. He pressed into the arch, dragging the towel upward in slow circles. My breath hitched. My legs kicked.

A soft, begging "no" slipped through my lips.

He paused, looking up at me. Annoyance flickered across his face, but the second his gaze landed on me, it vanished.

For a moment, he seemed just as unsure as I was, his hand hovering awkwardly with the towel.

I clamped my mouth shut, trying not to look like a complete mess.

He cleared his throat and lowered his head again.

His hand moved to my ankle and then my leg, holding me tighter this time, as if trying to strangle the moans in their crib. But it was no use, I started making soft noises as he wiped along my shin. By the time he reached my thighs, sweat had begun to form at my hairline.

"Can I... um.. have some water?" I asked, my mouth dry.

He ignored the request and flipped me onto my stomach. He dipped the towel back into the pot and placed it on my upper thigh. He wiped around carefully, and when it was done, he pushed the chair back and left the room.

When he returned, he had a glass of water in his hand.

He removed the towel and helped me up, then held the glass to my lips.

I drank.

As he placed the glass on the nightstand, I slid back down and lay flat, waiting for him to continue, which seemed to surprise him, because perhaps he had expected more resistance.

I watched him as he touched me. His hand was warm and broad, a little rough and covered in calluses. His grip was firm. His gaze, dark and unreadable.

I started to imagine myself as a deer, bound and captured, ready to bleed... for him.

It was the kind of thing that sounded terrifying in a story, but all I felt was a warm, thudding beat in my chest. A kind of fearlessness I had never experienced until now.

I wanted to be his prey, even if it would consume me.

I just knew — whatever kept me trapped in this cabin with him wasn't the cuffs or the four walls.

It was my hopeless affection.

The desperate desire to be fed, bathed, and fucked in his ways.

At last, he pulled the white dress over my head.

My heart fluttered when his eyes found me.

SEVEN

Another day went by.

He took a rifle from the wall and went out through the kitchen.

By the time he came back, he was holding two rabbits, dripping with blood. His eyes stopped on me for a long time when he saw me sitting in bed, wearing the dress he'd put on me that morning, looking at him like I'd been waiting for him this whole time.

His gaze tightened with desire. His Adam's apple dipped. He reached for his crotch to hide his reaction, but there was no hiding when it was just the two of us.

For a while, he stood there, unable to look away. My face burned, and yet my gaze stayed fierce, unavoidably fixed on him.

At last, he cleared his throat and raised the dead rabbits in his hand before escaping into the kitchen.

The next time he came into my room, he held a

cup of tea and a plate of honeycomb. He set them down and stirred the spoon in the tea.

He tested the temperature before feeding me.

Warmth spread from my stomach to the rest of my body, and somehow, his silence made all the feelings worse.

"Did you steal it from the bears?" I asked shyly, nodding toward the honeycomb.

"What?" he barked, a little annoyed.

"Nothing..." I shook my head.

He watched me with knotted brows, and after a while, he sighed.

His voice softened.

"Mike got me a big chunk in the summer," he said. "I sold most of it, but there's a little bit left. Thought you'd like it."

"I never had honeycomb before," I said.

"Never?" he sounded shocked.

I shook my head.

He rubbed his thumb on his index finger, as if he didn't know how to respond. At last, he picked the piece up and sent it between my lips.

"Well, try it. It's good for you."

I took a bite.

"Good?"

"Mm-hmm..."

"Take the rest." He pushed the piece back into my mouth.

A moan slipped from me, taken aback by how

rough he was. His fingers lingered in my mouth, and for a moment, instead of tasting the honey, I sucked on them, my knees closed tight.

And the air changed between us.

He pulled his fingers out and stood up.

The wood cracked in the kitchen, breaking the tension. When I looked up again, he was already holding the cup and plate, ready to leave.

"Stay with me..." I whispered, tracing the cuff with my finger.

He pretended not to hear me and left.

A while later, he returned with two bowls of rabbit soup. Instead of feeding me this time, he uncuffed me and pulled the chair beside me.

"Eat," he said, pressing the larger bowl into my hands, irritated by something.

I was sitting in a puddle, with my heart drumming like crazy. I had a feeling he should've continued what he'd been doing before he went into the kitchen... but perhaps he wasn't thinking that way.

He dug in, picking out the meat first, then chugging the broth. By the time he finished, I had barely touched mine.

He shot me a look, took his bowl into the kitchen, and returned with some bread. He sat next to me and sighed, breaking the bread and sending it to his mouth while I worked slowly on the soup.

My stomach was in knots, fully aware of the tension that had worsened during the day, so much so that no matter how hot and heavy his night visits were, it never eased.

We stayed in silence until he broke it with an impatient sigh.

"Quit playing with your food," he said with a stern voice.

I almost dropped the spoon.

He made a noise through the back of his nose. "Come sit on my lap."

He patted his leg and took the bowl from my hands.

I stood and climbed onto his lap. He wrapped an arm around me and held the spoon, scooping the rabbit meat to my lips. As I chewed, I started to feel a little needy on his lap.

He lifted the bowl and made me drink the rest. While I caught my breath, he broke some bread and held it to my lips.

I had my knees pressed together the whole time he fed me. At first, it felt innocent, but when he began to linger his fingers inside my mouth, I started making sucking noises, and the way he looked at me changed.

He fed me another piece, and even though I was no longer hungry, I took it. Heat pooled under my thighs. Something hard pressed against them.

There was no more bread, and it was just him holding me on his lap. My eyes fell to his lips beneath his newly groomed mustache.

A wild feeling rose. I leaned in and pressed my

lips to his. He hesitated, but only for a second. He grabbed the back of my head and gripped my hair, pulling me into him. I repositioned my legs on each side of him.

My tongue slid into his mouth. I purred, moving around his hardness like a fish. He bit my lips, sucked them, his hands roughing up my dress.

Heat rose between us dangerously.

He grabbed my hips and moved them up and down his cock with force, but when I was about to unbuckle his belt, he pushed me away.

He yanked my hair, pulling me off his lap, eyes blazing with anger.

"What the hell are you doing?"

"Kissing you..." My fingers curled in my lap.

"No!" he shouted, and it startled me.

His eyes flicked between me and himself, and the more he did, the more he seemed...repulsed by it.

"You don't do this," he muttered. "You just don't."

He stood abruptly and swept the chair aside. It hit the wall and crashed down. His eyes landed on the empty bowls, and his shoulders tensed.

He swept everything off the nightstand.

The bowls shattered.

The spoons bounced.

And finally, his eyes locked on me.

I bit my lips, hugging my arms, and his gaze flickered.

"You don't kiss me. Period," he said, as if he was

explaining something important. "That's not something you do."

"But I wanted to..." I murmured.

"What did you say?" His voice rose.

"I... wanted to kiss you..." I lowered my head, embarrassed that I could still say it.

"Well, don't."

He stepped toward me, grabbed me by the wrists, and dragged me back to the head of the bed, cuffing me there again.

This time, he brushed his thumb against the cuff instead of the back of my hand, and it made my heart ache.

"I'm not going to run," I muttered. "You know I'm not going anywhere."

He sighed, avoiding the words he didn't want to say.

"Maybe you should."

He stood and left.

A few minutes later, he walked back in. His eyes stopped on me briefly, seeing me still sitting on the edge of the bed exactly where he'd left me. He went into the bathroom for my toothbrush, toothpaste, and a cup, then into the kitchen for a bowl.

He wet my toothbrush, squeezed some toothpaste on it, then fed me some water.

"Open up," he said softly, crouching in front of me.

I felt his fingers grip my chin.

I avoided his gaze but obeyed. He reached in with

the toothbrush and brushed my teeth like I was a child, careful not to push too deep.

Afterward, he made me spit it out in the bowl, then stared at my face and wiped the toothpaste from the edge of my lips with his thumb, and it made my heart race.

EIGHT

"You can't be looking at me like that," he said with a soft voice that was hard to hear.

"Like what?"

"Like you have feelings for me."

"What if I do?" I bit my lip, feeling my heart racing again.

He drifted into silence again, and at last, I heard him sigh.

"Don't," he said. "You're gonna make this hard for both of us."

"Make what hard?" I frowned.

"You act like you don't know."

"Maybe I don't." I sighed. I felt like I was asking something I didn't want to hear.

But then, why was I asking at all?

"Every year, around the holiday season, I drive up and down this road. There's always a silly girl who could use some help in weather like this. She may not be alone. Sometimes, there are two of them. Sometimes, she has a boyfriend. But that's never a problem for me. So you gotta understand who you are to me."

"Casey," I reminded him.

"Sure," he said. "But it doesn't matter. To your folks, maybe. Not to me. To me, you're just the warm pussy I use for the next five months because there's no other warm pussy around. So every time you find yourself wet for me, think about that."

"My name is Casey..." I said it again, though it seemed to have no point.

He curled his lips, leaving me to process all this, and walked to the closet. From there, he took a red dress off the hanger.

"You're not walking away from this alive, sweetheart."

He sat down by my side and pulled the red dress over my head. He tucked a strand of hair behind my ear.

"This thing between us has an expiration date. The sooner you come to terms with it, the better it is for both of us."

"You keep saying that, but I don't understand..."

"Yes, you do." He zipped up my dress and pulled me to him, his hand rubbing my breasts. "I'm gonna kill you when spring comes, and I'm gonna enjoy every second of it."

"I'm not scared."

"You should."

He let go of me and put the cuffs back on my wrists, restraining me to the head of the bed.

This time, the cuffs really hurt. Pain settled in my bones. He didn't look at me again on his way out.

He slammed the door behind him and left me in my own room.

That night, he didn't pay me a visit.

I woke up three times, hoping to see him standing in his antler mask, but he didn't come.

As if he had forgotten about me...

The room went dark, and the logs turned cold.

The flames died.

And the room was cold.

My teeth chattered.

NINE

I found a scratched message on the wall among the tally of days. It looked as if someone had carved it with her nails.

It said,

"Don't run."

I didn't know what it meant.

Only that the bed frame had clearly been broken and put back together a few times. It wouldn't take much force to break again. The windows weren't barred, nor were they locked.

Everything I should know about him, I'd already known, so what should I do?

What would I do?

My eyes shifted outside the window.

My heart ached.

TEN

AT DAWN, I HEARD HIM COME INTO MY ROOM. HE took a sharp breath, realizing how cold it had gotten, but even then, he didn't stop by the hearth. He came straight to me, spread my curled legs, and pulled my trembling arms over my head. Then he lay his weight down on me, unzipping his pants.

His cock felt extra hot on my cold skin, and his touch warmed every inch of me.

I wanted to hate it, hate him, but I quivered and moaned, arching my back against his chest, craving the very person who'd be the end of me.

He locked me in his arms and pulled off his shirt. Then he pushed into me, deep and hot.

"Why are you still so wet for me?" he whispered breathlessly.

"I don't know..." I bit my lip, trying not to shiver so much.

His broad hands traced my skin. His lips brushed against my neck, and the heat of him enveloped me. He fucked me lovingly and roughly all at once, as if trying to warm me from the inside out. Soon, the chattering quieted.

My face flushed again. My body was drunk with sensation.

He had me pinned. Moans and grunts escaped his lips. And I was making slutty little noises. His touches felt intoxicatingly erotic. I was already close after a few thrusts, having ached for him a whole day. I tried to hold it in, not willing to give in too soon.

As if sensing how close I was, he quickened his pace, determined to force the truth out of me. He kept pushing harder and faster until I shattered underneath him.

He didn't stop.

He kept going, forcing tears from my eyes and cries from my lips. Then he turned me over for the first time, fucking me with his antlers pressed against my forehead.

He wrung another orgasm from me and spilled into me like a mess. Then he turned me around, parted my legs, removed his mask, and lowered his head. He held my hips to his face and ate my pussy until I came on his tongue.

And then he mounted me again from the back, harder and rougher this time, making me take his second load.

All night.
The fireplace remained dead.
But I was never cold.

ELEVEN

IT WAS AROUND THE FIFTH MONTH WHEN I started to show. My belly was visibly bigger than when I first met him, and the dress he handed to me had begun to feel a little tight around my waist.

I asked him for maternity clothes, but he told me he didn't have any and handed me a dress that didn't fit.

He stared at my belly sometimes, obsessed with the strain my body had put on the dress. At night, instead of fucking me in them, he'd rip them off and rub my swollen tits, grinding against me while I was still fully clothed. I'd come before he was even inside me. A few times, he barely got his cock out before spilling all over the place.

I didn't know what this was between us.

Just that it was there.

I took his antler in my mouth while he fucked me, cuffed to the bed.

He sat with me most of the time during the day and kissed me on the forehead before he left to hunt.

There was still no sight of spring.

For better and worse.

But we were both waiting for it. Just for vastly different reasons.

One day, he untied me from the bed and wrapped me in a coat and hat.

"Run," he said. "I'm letting you go. Make your way out of the woods, and you'll be free."

He pushed me through the kitchen door and pointed at his footsteps leading into the mountains. "If you keep going that way, you'll make it out in two days."

"What if I freeze to death?"

"You want me to pack you some food? Hot-water bag?" he raised his voice. "Is that it?"

I nodded, then shook my head.

He sighed and went back into the kitchen to grab a few pieces of deer jerky. He tucked them into my pocket and pushed me outside, then shut the door behind me.

I walked a few steps, then circled back and banged on the door.

He opened it after a moment.

He held my face with both hands, making me look him in the eye.

"Casey," he said, calling me by my name for the first time. "Listen to me."

I swallowed.

"If you stay here with me, I will kill both you and the child."

"Our child," I whispered, biting my lip.

"Find yourself a good man. Hm? The kind who doesn't go crazy in the woods."

I shook my head.

"Come on!"

He grabbed an axe and shouted, startling me. My hand went to my belly as I backed away.

He looked at me with something dark and wicked in his eyes.

I didn't want to leave, but my survival instinct made me turn and start walking.

Tears rolled down my cheeks.

I kept turning my head to look at him. He just stood there, holding that axe, a deeply conflicted look on his face.

I started running.

I tried not to look back, but in the end, I couldn't help it.

I didn't really want to go.

Killer or not.

Crazy man in the mountains or not.

So I stopped.

I turned back.

And there he was, standing between the trees with a rifle, aiming at me.

The loose restraint. The poorly guarded room. The lack of maternity clothes.

He wasn't waiting for spring.

He was waiting for me to escape so he could hunt me, like he had done to the others.

Pain cut through my heart.

He pulled the trigger.

The crack of the rifle echoed.

Snow fell.

White smoke drifted from the barrel.

A bullet slammed into the tree trunk beside me.

Tears rushed to my eyes.

But I was...unharmed.

He lowered the rifle, slung it over his shoulder, and walked back into the cabin.

Alone and silent.

Just the way he had been for the past few months.

And I knew it was over.

He let me go.

But I... I couldn't.

Even after everything, I couldn't.

I was... gasping and crying, running knee-deep in the snow back to the cabin where we had spent the last five months together.

The kitchen door was open, and he was sitting there with his rifle in his arms, eyes staring blankly at the wall. He hadn't expected me to come back.

He stood up the minute I showed up at the door.

Without another word, he pulled me toward him and bit me hard on the lips. I felt dizzy and stumbled, and my back hit the wall. He pressed me deeper into it, stealing my breath. His hands worked my dress up, then he turned me around and pressed me against his chest.

His hand was on my belly.

"Silly girl." He grabbed a handful of my hair while feeling my baby bump.

"Silly, pregnant girl." He kissed my neck.

"My big bad wolf..." I touched his fingers, lost in his touch.

"I don't even have pregnant woman clothes for you."

"Your shirts will do." I bit his lips.

"You're fucking crazy..."

"Just crazy about you."

I moaned, unbuckling his pants.

He let me take him in my hand, eager and wet.

"If you're gonna stay, we're gonna have a few rules."

"Okay."

"I'm not gonna stop." He slammed into me, a fistful of my hair in his hand, as he said it in a harsh whisper. "Death turns me on. It still does."

"Then I'll be your little Red Riding Hood to carry the bloodline."

His hand reached for my swollen waist again, and I felt his hips twitch.

"You're so fucking pregnant."

Snow fell from the roof. I gasped.

From the moment I arrived, I knew I was never meant to leave.

THE END, UNTIL IT'S NOT

KEEP READING…

PRETTY GIRL: A DARK WEB THRILLER

00:00:00

[LIVESTREAM 304]
08:00 AM CT | STATUS: LIVE FEED ACTIVE
— BID OPEN
VIEWERS: 1,294

[ANNIEWALKERS88]: Been waiting weeks
for this one. First cry on me — 10
[CRYBABY2345]: new girl's pretty. I'd
say the blindfold comes off — 22
[ANONYMOUSMEMBER10]: blindfold stays
on — 100
[ANONYMOUSMEMBER040]: 50 for red
[CRYBABY2345] 10 — gag off
[ANONYMOUSMEMBER10]: 101 for the gag

[CRYBABY2345]: 102 — the gag is mine…
[SYSTEM NOTICE]: COUNTDOWN BEGINS. 12
HOURS REMAINING.

…

Get Pretty Girl now on Amazon | Website

FROM THE AUTHOR

If you enjoyed this book, spread the word and don't be shy.

Sign up for my newsletter to get notified about discounts, ARC opportunities, unfiltered editions, bonus chapters, and more exclusive content: https://www.thepunkhead.com/book-signup-form

His Winter Baby will be included in my untitled, forthcoming serial-killer box set.

ALSO BY KATRINA YANG

My Latex Obsession

Saved by a serial killer, she becomes part of his doll collection...

Little Lamb

At a Christmas party, two pairs of eyes lock across the room. Told from the POV of an unreliable narrator, Little Lamb isn't the story you think it is.